This book belongs to:

....

To Justin. Sleep peacefully. A.S.

For the very patient Spencer, Theo and Tegan. L.M.

OXFORD
UNIVERSITY PRESS

Great Clarendon Street, Oxford OX2 6DP
Oxford University Press is a department of the University of Oxford.
It furthers the University's objective of excellence in research, scholarship,
and education by publishing worldwide. Oxford is a registered trade mark of
Oxford University Press in the UK and in certain other countries

First published in 2011
This edition first published in 2018

British Library Cataloguing in Publication Data
Data available

ISBN: 978-0-19-276854-4

10 9 8 7 6 5 4 3 2 1

Printed in China

Paper used in the production of this book is a natural,
recyclable product made from wood grown in sustainable forests.
The manufacturing process conforms to the environmental
regulations of the country of origin.

My First Milestones

How Many Sleeps?

Amber Stewart • Layn Marlow

OXFORD
UNIVERSITY PRESS

Toast woke early one morning.
He knew that something exciting was going
to happen, and it was going to happen soon.

He could smell it in the quiet morning air,
in the mist still hugging the ground,
in the autumn leaves trembling on
the branches ready to tumble
a golden blanket over the wood.

Toast watched, waiting for
the first leaf to fall . . .

because when the first leaf fell,
that meant it was nearly his birthday.

'How many sleeps till
my birthday?' he asked,
as Mummy tucked him in.

'Too many to start
counting now,'
smiled Mummy.

'How many sleeps till my birthday?'
Toast asked the next night,
and the next,

until one night Mummy said,
'Just enough sleeps to deliver
party invitations to all
your friends.'

So the next day that is exactly what they did.

They delivered
invitations all the way
from Little Hollow . . .

to Big Oak Tree . . .

to Rabbit, Mole, and
Squirrel Red Tail.

'How many sleeps till my birthday now, Mummy?' murmured Toast, so tired from his long walk.

'Just enough sleeps to go collecting party treats,' whispered Mummy.

After breakfast, they gathered
armfuls of gold and rubies, and
special leaves for wrapping.

'How many sleeps till my birthday,
from this exact moment?' Toast wondered,
right in the middle of his bedtime story.

'Exactly enough sleeps to help
Mummy decorate the cake,' said Daddy.

In the morning, Mummy and Toast
picked petals and berries
and nuts for the cake.

Then together they decorated it
so that it was the best birthday cake
Toast had ever seen.

In bed, each evening, Toast lay dreaming
of invitation delivering, of party treats,
of birthday cake, and of what his
present might be.

And each evening Daddy wondered,
quite worriedly, 'How many more
sleeps until Toast's birthday?'

'Just enough, I'm sure,'
Mummy always said,
secretly crossing her fingers.

'Guess how many sleeps now, Toast?'
said Mummy one morning.
'How many?' wailed Daddy.

'Just enough to wrap the party treats,
put the candles on the cake,
and get an extra special early night . . .'

'But that means —' squeaked Toast,
'that means — my birthday is tomorrow!'

And it was.

And there was easily enough time to love
the gifts, play the party games, and eat up
all the cake. And, best of all . . .

time for Toast to open a very special present

and let all his friends share in the fun.

When Toast's day had drawn to an
end — and he was giving Daddy
a hug — he whispered dreamily,
'How many sleeps till my next birthday?'

'Just enough sleeps for Daddy
to start on your next present,'
Mummy whispered back.

But Toast was already asleep.

Ten Top Tips

Here are some hints and tips for preparing your toddler's birthday party so that it goes off just as well as Toast's party in this story.

1 Think about how many children to invite — you'll know whether your toddler is happy in a smaller or larger group.

2 Consider making hand-made invitations together — you'll enjoy the creative, quality time!

3 If all the party guests are about the same age it can make things go more smoothly.

4 Name badges can be helpful!

5 Don't make the party last too long or start it too late in the afternoon. You don't want tired and grumpy guests!

6 Prepare what you need for some simple party games and remember to have a supply of small gifts or treats that you can award as prizes.

7 Choose bite-sized portions of party food as excited children usually don't have much of an appetite!

8 Children love make-believe so having a party theme and asking children to come in fancy dress is a great idea for a toddler birthday celebration.

9 In case of any accidents amid the excitement, have some spare clothes to hand.

10 Pencils, stickers, and activity sheets work well in party bags when it's time to go home.